USBORNE HOTSHOTS
MAGIC TRICKS

USBORNE HOTSHOTS
MAGIC TRICKS

Edited by Gina Walker
Designed by Karen Tomlins

Illustrated by Kim Blundell, John Davey,
Chris Lyon, Joseph McEwan, Martin
Newton, Kim Raymond, Paul Sullivan
and Ian Thompson

Series editor: Judy Tatchell
Series designer: Ruth Russell

CONTENTS

About magic

Magic is fun to perform as well as fun to watch. There are lots of different kinds of magic acts. This book is full of tricks for different acts.

Close-up magic is performed for small audiences, using props the magicians carry with them.

Cabaret magic acts, with elaborate costumes and props, are often seen on television.

Mentalism involves feats of the mind, like reading people's minds, or bending forks.

For **children's magic**, the magician uses bright, cheerful props, and often dresses up.

Props

Things you use in a performance are called props (short for properties). You can use everyday things – magic with familiar objects can be more impressive than with special magic props. Be imaginative. Instead of a ball, use an orange, for instance. Or choose props with a theme, such as a Chinese theme.

Use bright new coins, not dull or tarnished ones.

New playing cards, that slip well, are easiest to handle.

Magic skills

There are some skills and techniques that are used in many tricks. In this book, the symbol above shows where a skill is explained. Two very useful skills are described below.

Magician's Choice

Magician's Choice is a technique used in many tricks. Your volunteer seems to choose an item freely, but you manipulate what she says so she "chooses" the one you want.

1. You want the volunteer to choose the yellow square. Ask her to point to a square.

2. If she points to the yellow one, you can say the yellow one is her choice.

3. If she points to the red one, don't panic. Stay calm and continue without hesitating.

4. Say the volunteer has ruled out the red one, leaving yellow as her choice.

In some tricks, the volunteer chooses between three items. You may need to use Magician's Choice twice to get the right item chosen. Be confident, and no one will question you.

Misdirection

Misdirection is a very important skill in magic. It involves subtly directing the audience's attention away from what you are doing. For example, when you are making a secret move, you can misdirect by hiding it with an obvious move. Repeat the obvious move a few times before you make the secret move. Then people will not be watching so closely.

Your eyes tell people where to look. Never look in the direction of the real action or object.

Talk to divert attention away from your hands.

Always have a believable reason for each move you make.

Changes of pace look suspicious. Try to keep a smooth speed.

Magic with cards

Playing cards are used in magic tricks more than any other prop. To do card tricks well, you will need lots of practice. The next eight pages show you some handling skills, and lots of tricks in which to use them.

Overhand Shuffle

Shuffling disturbs the order of the pack.

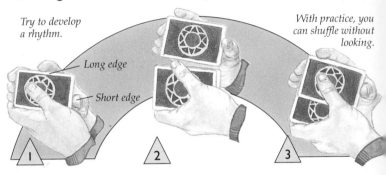

Try to develop a rhythm.

With practice, you can shuffle without looking.

Long edge

Short edge

1 Rest the pack on the long edge, in one hand. Hold the short edges with the fingers and thumb of your other hand.

2 Lift the pack with the upper hand, while pressing with your other thumb to draw some cards into your lower hand.

3 Lift the pack over the drawn-off cards. Repeat 2 and 3 until all the cards are in your lower hand. Square (straighten up) the pack.

Countdown trick

1 Ask someone to pick a card. Shuffle Control it to the top (see page 7). Ask for any number between 5 and 15.

2 Deal out that many cards, face-down. Turn the last card, and say this is the chosen card. It is not, so look puzzled.

Cutting the cards

Unlike shuffling, cutting the pack does not disturb the order of the cards. Below you can see how to do the Kick Cut. Begin by holding the pack face-down on the table.

With your right first finger, lift about half the cards.

Swivel the lifted cards, pivoting on your thumb.

Take the lifted cards, and put the lower cards on top.

Shuffle Control

A control brings a chosen card to the top of the pack.

Get someone to pick out a card. Start an Overhand Shuffle with the pack. Stop and have the card placed on top of your lower hand.

Now shuffle a single card into your lower hand. Let it fall out of line so it sticks out a little in your direction. This is "in-jogging".

Shuffle the rest of the cards. People will not see the in-jogged card. Cut the cards below it to the top of the pack. The chosen card is now on top.

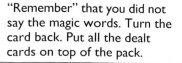

"Remember" that you did not say the magic words. Turn the card back. Put all the dealt cards on top of the pack.

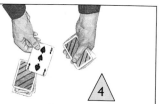

Say some magic words. Ask the volunteer to deal out the right number of cards. The last card dealt is the chosen card.

More magic with cards

Here are some more card skills, and a trick which uses them all.

Classic Spread

Draw your hands apart.

The cards spread one under the other.

1. Hold the pack in one hand. Push a few cards at a time into the other, with your thumb.

2. Spread the cards into a line or fan. Support them with your fingers underneath.

Thumb Fan

Hold the pack between thumb and palm. Push your thumb against the bottom cards at the top edge.

Curve your thumb across the tops of the cards. If the cards slip well, they will swivel into a fan.

If your hands seem too small at first, keep trying!

The Glimpse

The Glimpse is important in many card tricks. It is a way of seeing the bottom card in the pack, without people noticing.

1. Shuffle, and as you square the pack, turn it to face you very slightly.

2. Glance at the bottom card, and remember it.

Key Card Control

This is another way of getting a chosen card to the top.

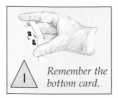

Remember the bottom card.

Chosen card

Chosen card

Shuffle, square the pack, and Glimpse the bottom card. This is the key card.

Spread or Fan the pack. Ask someone to choose a card and remember it.

Gather up the pack, with the chosen card to one side, face-down.

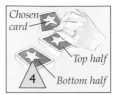

Chosen card

Top half

Bottom half

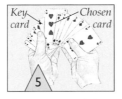

Key card

Chosen card

Cut the pack. Ask the volunteer to put the chosen card on the top half, and complete the cut.

Cut again, and then spread the pack face-up. The chosen card is on top of the key card, on its right.

Cut the chosen card and those to its right, to the top. The chosen card is on top of the pack.

Choose your card

Use steps 1 to 3 of the Key Card Control, then follow these steps.

1. Cut the pack, and get the chosen card placed on top of the top half. Cut again.

2. Search the pack. Take the key card, and the two next to it. Place them face-down.

Key card

3. Use Magician's Choice (page 5) to make the volunteer pick the chosen card, in the middle.

Chosen card

9

Trickier tricks

So far, most tricks in this book have been self-working. That means they do not need any secret moves, or sleights. The skills and tricks on the next four pages do involve sleights. You may find them difficult at first, but keep trying.

The Glide

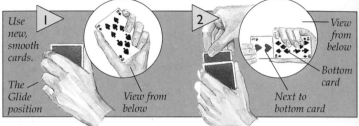

Use new, smooth cards.

The Glide position

View from below

View from below

View from below

Bottom card

Next to bottom card

Gliding is taking the next to bottom card in the pack, but seeming to take the bottom one. Hold the pack face-down as shown. Curl your second and third fingers under to get a grip on the bottom card.

Now do the Glide. As you reach to take a card with your other hand, pull the bottom card back with your second and third fingers. Take the next to bottom card. Then slide the bottom card back into place.

Double Lift

Double Lifting is showing the second to top card in the pack, but seeming to show the top one.

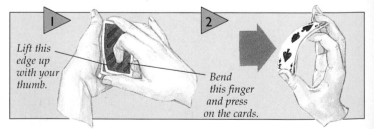

Lift this edge up with your thumb.

Bend this finger and press on the cards.

Take the pack in one hand. Hold the short edges with the fingers and thumb of the other.

With this thumb, carefully bend up the top two cards and Double Lift them as one.

One in three

Deal from the bottom, in the Glide position. Ask someone to say when to stop.

Stop dealing. Show your volunteer the bottom card in the pack. Ask him to remember it.

Glide out the next to bottom card. The volunteer thinks it is his card. "Lose" the card in the pack.

After this step, chosen card is next to bottom of pack.

Glide out a card. Say "One deal later, and this would have been your card." Put it on the bottom.

Show the top dealt card. Say, "One deal sooner, this would be the card." Put the dealt pile on top.

Say you will find the card. Cut the pack in three. Put one third on each side of the first pile.

Show the bottom card of the left pile. Ask if it is the card. It is not, so look puzzled. Place the card face-down. Put the pile aside.

Show the bottom of the middle pile. Ask again. When he says "No", Glide out a card and lay it face down to the right of the first card.

Repeat 7 for the final pile. Place the bottom card to the right of the others. Use Magician's Choice to get the middle card chosen.

11

Slips, switches and palms

Here are some more card sleights, and tricks which use them.

The Backslip

The Backslip is a way of cutting the pack to get the top card on top of the bottom half.

Left side

Hold the pack in the left hand. Lift the left side of the top half with the right hand.

Pull the top card onto the lower half with your left fingers.

Slide the card off smoothly.

As you slide the top card off, turn your left palm down to hide the move.

Card switch

If number is six, chosen card is sixth in pack.

Volunteer

Chosen card is now fifth.

Ask for a number from 5 to 15. Show the top 15 cards. Say "Remember the one at your number".

Replace the cards on the pack. Cut the pack, and Backslip the top card onto the bottom half.

Give the volunteer the top half of the pack. Keep the rest. Ask her to check her card is still there.

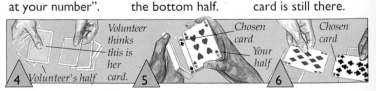

Volunteer thinks this is her card.

Volunteer's half

Chosen card

Your half

Chosen card

Ask what number she chose. Deal that many cards less one, from her half onto your cards.

Say you will pick out the chosen card by cutting your half of the pack. Do another Backslip.

Ask the volunteer to turn her top card, and you turn yours. Your top card is her chosen card.

The Palm

Palming a card is hiding it in the palm of your hand.

1. Hold the pack in your left hand with your thumb slightly bent, as shown here.

Your right hand hides this move.

2. Straighten your thumb, pushing out the top card. Move your right hand to take the pack.

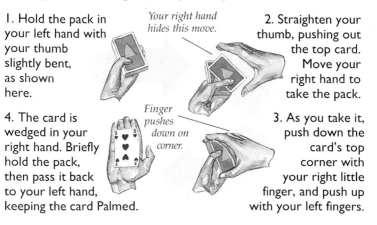

4. The card is wedged in your right hand. Briefly hold the pack, then pass it back to your left hand, keeping the card Palmed.

Finger pushes down on corner.

3. As you take it, push down the card's top corner with your right little finger, and push up with your left fingers.

Pocket the card

First ask someone to think of a number from 1 to 10.

Show the first ten cards in the pack, one at a time. Ask the volunteer to remember the card at his number.

Chosen card

Say you will now find his card. Take a card from just below ten down. Look at it, frown, and put it on top of the pack.

Repeat step 2, but this time smile and pocket the card. Ask the number, and deal the volunteer this many cards, face-down.

Palm the card on top of the pack. Ask the volunteer to see if the new top card is the one he chose.

Palmed card is the chosen card.

When he says "No", reply "Of course not. Your card is here." Reach into your pocket and produce the Palmed card.

13

Money magic

To be able to do coin tricks really well, you must first master some coin sleights. The next four pages show you some sleights, and some tricks that use them.

Finger Palm

"Palming" a coin is a way of hiding it in your hand, so the audience thinks it has vanished. To Finger Palm a coin, bend your two middle fingers and hold the coin in them. Let the other fingers curl naturally.

Classic Palm

The Classic Palm is the best way of hiding a coin, but the hardest to do. Press the coin into your palm with your two middle fingers. Push across the fleshy base of your thumb to hold it. Straighten your fingers.

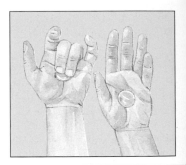

Coin illusion trick

1

For this trick you need three coins. Start with one coin Classic Palmed in your hand.

2

Hold two other coins between your finger and thumb. Say you will make an extra coin appear.

Tear the coin

For this trick you need a coin and a square of
paper 10cm x 10cm (4in x 4in).

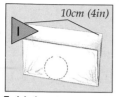

Fold the paper so
one side is 2.5cm
(1in) shorter than
the other. Drop the
coin into the fold.

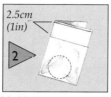

Hold the paper with
the short side in
your direction, and
fold the sides back
behind the coin.

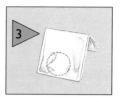

Fold the top over,
to make a pocket.
The top edge is
open, but nobody
should notice.

Hold the pocket at
the open edge. Tap
the pocket on the
table to prove the
coin is still inside.

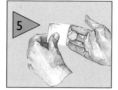

Take the pocket in
your left hand,
letting the coin slip
out into your right.
Finger Palm the coin.

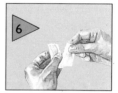

Say the coin has
vanished, and tear
up the pocket. Later,
drop the coin safely
into your pocket.

Rub the two coins quickly back
and forth, like this. There seem
to be three coins, not two.

When the audience claim it is
just an optical illusion, throw all
three coins on the table.

Vanishing cash

Thumb Palm

The Thumb Palm is another way of holding a coin
invisibly. To produce the coin again, reverse the steps.

Hold the coin flat
between your first
and second fingers.

Curl the coin into
the crook of your
thumb, like this.

Pinch it between your
thumb and palm. The
coin has vanished!

Top pocket vanish

For this trick, you must wear a shirt with a pocket. First, show a
coin. Pretend to take it in your left hand, but French Drop it into
your right (page 17), and Thumb Palm it. Then go on as follows.

*A hankie in
the pocket
will help
hold it
open, and
hide the drop.*

Say the coin will move from
your left hand, up your left arm
and across into your right hand.

Trace the path of the coin with
your right hand. As you pass the
pocket, smoothly drop the coin.

Pretend to make the coin move
as described, following the path
with your eyes. Open your right
hand. The coin is not there.

Seem puzzled. The audience will
assume the coin is still in your
left hand. Open that too, to
show the coin has vanished.

French Drop vanish

The French Drop is a very useful sleight for making small props seem to disappear. In this trick, you make a coin disappear, using several different techniques to misdirect the audience.

To misdirect, keep looking at the wand.

Place a coin and a magic wand on a table. (You could use a pencil instead of a wand.) Take the coin between the thumb and first finger of your right hand, and show it to the audience.

Now look at the wand on the table as if you want to pick it up, but you cannot because you have the coin in your right hand. This gives you a good reason to make the next move, in Step 3.

Put your left hand over your right hand, and pretend to take the coin in your left hand. Instead, drop it back into your right hand. This is called a French Drop. Keep looking at the wand to misdirect.

Audience looks where you look.

Close your left hand, and pick up the wand with your right hand, still holding the coin. Now look at your left hand, where the coin is meant to be. The audience will follow your eyes.

Look at your left fist, and tap it with the wand, as if working magic. (The "magic" was really in Step 3. This time delay also helps to misdirect.) The audience still assumes the coin is in your left hand.

Open your empty left hand, and show it with a flourish, amazed that the coin has gone. People will respond to your reaction. Later, subtly drop the coin from your right hand into your pocket.

Dicey tricks

The next four pages show some tricks using everyday things like dice, rubber bands and matches.

The Paddle Move

The Paddle Move appears to change the numbers on a dice.

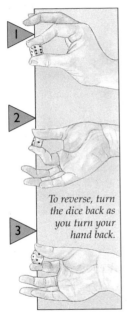

1 Hold a dice between your first finger and your thumb, with the 6 facing you and the 3 on the face to the left of the 6, as you look at it. Make sure the audience sees the 6 clearly.

2 Now, turn your hand to show the audience the face opposite the 6, which is the 1. Turn your hand back, and show the 6. Repeat this once or twice, so people are sure the opposite face is 1.

To reverse, turn the dice back as you turn your hand back.

3 Turn your hand again, but twist the dice round by one face at the same time, in the same direction as your hand, so now the 2 faces you. The 1 appears to have changed to a 2. This is the Paddle Move.

Dice count

Ask a volunteer to roll two dice, while you turn your back. Ask him to double the number on one, then add 5, multiply by 5, and add the other dice number. Ask him the total.

$2 \times 2 = 4$
$4 + 5 = 9$
$9 \times 5 = 45$

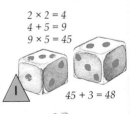

$45 + 3 = 48$

Subtract 25 from the total. You will get a two-figure number. The first figure is the dice number he originally doubled. The second figure is the other dice number. "Magically" reveal his numbers.

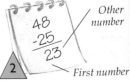

Other number

48
−25
23

First number

Three dice trick

Before you start this trick, moisten your thumb and first finger. Don't let anyone see you do this. Now hold three dice firmly between your thumb and first finger.

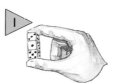

People may try to copy you but they will not succeed because they do not know your secret!

Release the pressure of your fingers on the dice a little. The middle dice should fall out, while the other two stick between your fingers, as if by magic.

Dice roll

2 + 6 + 5 = 13

Turn your back, asking a volunteer to roll three dice and add up the numbers.

Turned over

13 + 5 = 18

Ask her to turn any one dice upside-down, and add the new number to her total.

Rolled again

18 + 4 = 22

Now ask her to roll this dice again, and add this third number to the total.

Magician's sum
6 + 5 + 4 + 7
= 22

Turning back, silently add the numbers showing. Add 7 to get your volunteer's total.

Boxes and bands

Magic matchbox

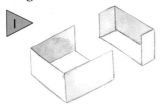

To prepare this trick, cut a piece off the end of an empty matchbox tray, about a quarter of the way along.

Put the tray pieces back into the cover. Mark the end of the long piece. Replace the matches, with their heads at the marked end.

To start, hold the box with the mark on top. Pull up the top end, while seeming to push up the bottom. The box is empty.

Push the top end back in. Now push up the bottom end properly, to open the box. The matches magically reappear.

Snap band

This trick is hard to get right, but worth the effort.

1 *Use a large band.*

Loop the band around your right thumb and first finger. Take the middle of the band with your left hand.

2 *The band crosses over in the middle.* Loop

Slip the loop from your right thumb onto your right finger. Put all your right fingers into that side of the loop.

3 *The ends of the double band meet in a "knot".* Loop

Take a firm hold of the "knot" between your left first finger and thumb, like this. Put all your left fingers into the loop.

Escaping match

To prepare, slide a match between the cover and tray of a full matchbox, facing the same way as the ones inside.

Show all sides of the closed box. Remove the cover with one hand, holding the tray and match underneath with the other.

Carefully replace the cover, holding the match with your thumb, like this. Make sure the match stays outside the cover.

Hold the box over a volunteer's hand, and tap it, letting the match fall. The match seems to have escaped through the box.

Keep the band stretched to look like a single thickness.

Knot

Take your right first finger out of the loop, and use it and your thumb to hold the band close to your left hand.

The ends of the doubled band snap apart.

Keep the double loop stretched tight, and pull your hands apart. The band will make a convincing snapping sound.

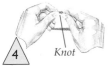

Show the "snapped" band, and then gather it into your hand. Make a magic gesture, and show the "mended" band.

Cabaret magic

In cabaret, an entertaining presentation is as important as technical skill. Try the tricks on the next four pages, and think of your own ways of presenting them.

Afghan bands

In this trick, you cut apparently identical loops of paper, but get different results. You could ask a helper to cut twisted loops while you cut plain ones, and joke that he or she can't get it right.

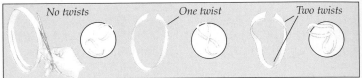
No twists   One twist   Two twists

Glue a paper strip in a plain loop. When you cut it like this, you get two loops.

If you twist once as you glue the loop, you get one long loop when you cut.

If you make two twists in the loop, you get two loops linked up, by "magic".

Rope trick

For this trick, you need a rope about 1.5m (5ft) long.

1

Hold the rope near one end (called end A here), between finger and thumb.

2

Place the other end (B) next to A, also sticking up above your hand a little.

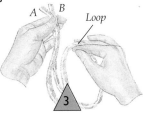

Loop

3

With your right first and second fingers, lift the bottom of the loop of rope.

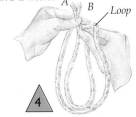

A   B   Loop

4

Put your right thumb through the loop. Grab end B below your left thumb.

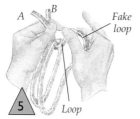

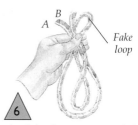

Pull some rope through the loop with your right hand, making a fake loop.

Take the fake loop in your left hand. Use your thumb to hide where the ropes meet.

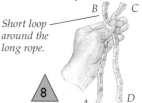

Short loop around the long rope.

Cut the fake loop with sharp scissors. Now you have four ends, A, B, C and D.

Drop ends A and D. Now you seem to have two pieces of rope hanging down.

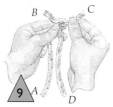

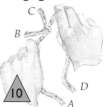

Say you will make the two pieces into one again. Tie a knot with ends B and C.

A knot is not a very magical way of joining ropes. Say you will get rid of it.

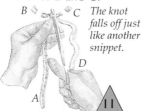

The knot falls off just like another snippet.

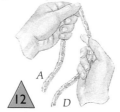

Hide the knot with your left hand. Snip off the short ends, then the knot itself.

Take end D in your right hand. Pull the rope through to show it is one piece again.

More cabaret magic

Coin in string trick

For this trick you will need some string or yarn, a tumbler, and a tube of cardboard. It helps if the tumbler is decorated or patterned, so it is harder to see through.

This end is left open.

Totally cover this end.

Don't wind the string too tight.

To prepare the trick, roll a piece of cardboard about 8cm x 4cm (3in x 1½in) into a tube. Overlap the ends by about 1cm (½in), and stick them together with glue or tape. Paint the tube to match your string. Then hold the tube on one finger and wind string around it until it looks like a normal ball of string.

Mark the coin, to prove it is the same one.

1 Show the tumbler with the string on top. The open end of the tube is down so it cannot be seen.

2 Borrow a coin. Make it vanish using a Thumb Palm (page 16). Take the string in your left hand.

3 Place the string in your right hand, with the open end of the tube over the Palmed coin.

Squeeze the string to keep coin inside.

Keep watching your left hand.

Volunteer

4 Turn the tumbler, to show it is empty. Casually turn the string, so the coin drops into the tube.

5 Pull out the tube on your right thumb, like this. The coin stays in the string. Palm the tube.

6 Balance the string on the tumbler. As a volunteer unwinds it, the coin will drop into the glass.

Hankie vanish

The volunteer assumes this is the real coin.

1. Prepare a hankie by opening the hem at one corner, and inserting a coin. Then sew the hem up again.

2. To start, hide the coin corner in your left hand. Hold a similar coin in your right hand, and drape the hankie over it.

3. Take the coin corner up under the hankie. Thumb Palm the real coin in your right hand (page 16).

4. Ask a volunteer to hold the sewn-in coin through the hankie. Whisk the hankie away, and the coin vanishes.

Rope escape

For this trick, you need a scarf, a rope, a helper and a screen.

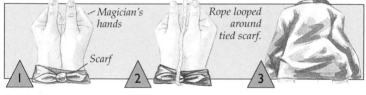

Magician's hands
Scarf
Rope looped around tied scarf.

1. As the helper ties your wrists with the scarf, twist them subtly to keep a little room between them.

2. Get your helper to loop the rope between your arms and hold both ends, standing a little away.

3. Hide your hands in some way. On stage, you could use a screen, but a jacket works just as well.

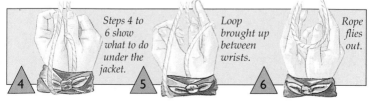

Steps 4 to 6 show what to do under the jacket.
Loop brought up between wrists.
Rope flies out.

4. Wriggle your hands to bring the loop of rope up through the scarf, and between your wrists.

5. Quickly work the loop of rope up and over one hand. Let the rope fall slack to the outside.

6. Now jerk your hands back sharply. The rope slips under the scarf, and you escape with hands still tied!

All in the mind

Mentalists seem to use mind reading, telepathy and other mental powers. You need a confident style and a knack for quick thinking.

Newspaper prediction

In this trick you "predict" where a volunteer will tell you to cut a newspaper column. It is best not to be too close to the audience.

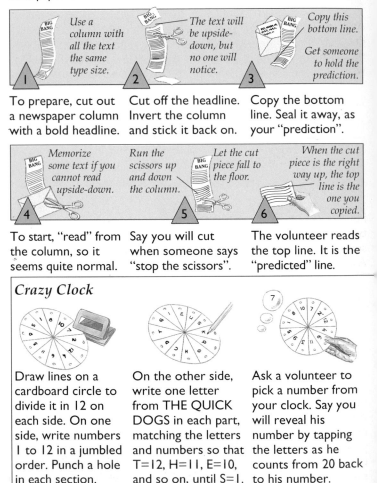

1. *Use a column with all the text the same type size.*

To prepare, cut out a newspaper column with a bold headline.

2. *The text will be upside-down, but no one will notice.*

Cut off the headline. Invert the column and stick it back on.

3. *Copy this bottom line.*

Get someone to hold the prediction.

Copy the bottom line. Seal it away, as your "prediction".

4. *Memorize some text if you cannot read upside-down.*

To start, "read" from the column, so it seems quite normal.

5. *Run the scissors up and down the column. Let the cut piece fall to the floor.*

Say you will cut when someone says "stop the scissors".

6. *When the cut piece is the right way up, the top line is the one you copied.*

The volunteer reads the top line. It is the "predicted" line.

Crazy Clock

Draw lines on a cardboard circle to divide it in 12 on each side. On one side, write numbers 1 to 12 in a jumbled order. Punch a hole in each section.

On the other side, write one letter from THE QUICK DOGS in each part, matching the letters and numbers so that T=12, H=11, E=10, and so on, until S=1.

Ask a volunteer to pick a number from your clock. Say you will reveal his number by tapping the letters as he counts from 20 back to his number.

26

Personality probe

Don't take more than ten names.

Don't let the audience see the names.

To misdirect, ask someone to repeat a name, or spell it.

1 Ask for some famous names. Pretend to write each on a separate piece of paper. Instead, write the first name each time.

2 Say you will predict which will be picked out of all the names. Write the first name again, and seal in an envelope.

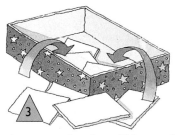

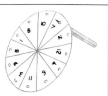

3 Put the papers in a box. Take two, "read" out two names suggested earlier, and replace. Ask a volunteer to pick one.

4 Ask the volunteer to read the chosen name, and then read your "prediction". The names are the same.

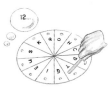

Turn the card letter-side-up. Ask the volunteer to count back from 20 by one number each time you tap a letter. At his number, he must say "stop".

Tap letters at random for the first eight taps. For the ninth, tap the letter T. Then tap the letters in order, spelling out THE QUICK DOGS.

When he says "stop", push the pencil through the hole in the section you are on. Show him the other side, which shows his chosen number.

Party tricks

With children's party tricks, having fun and letting children join in are more important than doing elaborate tricks.

Farmyard fun

Make six cards, like those below. There are two cow cards. One is a double-facer, with a horse on the back. The others have a house on the back. Pile the cards face up in the order shown. Pin the one-sided cow card to your back.

"?" card

You could draw pictures, or cut them out of magazines.

Daisy the cow – double-facer card.

Pin this card to your back.

Horse card

Back of "?" card

Back of double-facer.

1 Show the horse card on top. Ask the children to make a horse noise. Put the horse at the back.

2 Do the same for the pig and sheep. Then show the cow. Say Daisy is shy and might turn her back.

3 Do a Double Lift (see page 10). Turn both Daisy and the "?" card around and replace on the pack.

This is the double-facer.

4 Turn the top card. The "?" card shows instead of Daisy. She seems to have gone.

5 Look around for Daisy. The children will see Daisy on your back, and shout out.

6 Pretend not to understand. Call for Daisy. In the end, "find" the card.

Silk scarves

For this trick you need four silk scarves: a medium-sized red one, a medium-sized yellow one, a large one that is half red and half yellow, and a small one that is half red and half yellow. You could buy these at a magic shop, or dye some white scarves yourself.

It looks like two scarves tied together.

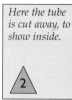

Here the tube is cut away, to show inside.

To prepare, tie the small yellow and red scarf loosely around the middle of the large scarf.

Hide the knotted scarves in the tube, red half near the top, yellow half near the bottom.

To present the trick, show the tube and the two medium scarves. Tie the two scarves together.

This seems like the other end of the medium scarves.

Turning the tube is not very magical!

Stuff the medium scarves into the tube, red end at the top, and yellow end at the bottom.

Push down the hidden scarves, and pull out the yellow corner. Leave some red at the top.

Say the scarves will magically change ends. With a flourish turn the tube around. There will be groans.

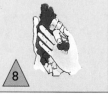

Scarves appear joined!

As "a better trick", push the red end into the tube. Pull the yellow end and remove the big scarf.

Crumple it in your hands, secretly undoing the small scarf and Palming it (pages 14 and 16).

Take a wand from your pocket. Leave the small scarf there. Wave the wand and open the big scarf.

More party tricks

See page 14 for how to Palm a coin.

Coin in roll

Finding a coin in a bread roll is a good trick for parties. Start with a coin Palmed in your hand.

View from underneath

Press in your thumbs to break the roll open underneath.

Press up with your fingers, pushing the Palmed coin inside.

Break open the top of the roll, to show the coin.

Vanishing grape

In this trick you make a grape vanish and reappear in your mouth. At parties, it looks good to use fruit from a bowl on the table.

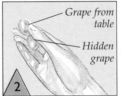

Grape from table

Hidden grape

Finger Palm a grape in your right hand (page 14), and have another grape ready on a table.

Pick up the grape from the table as shown, so the hidden grape is behind the visible one.

Put both grapes in your mouth, leaving the second one sticking out. It looks like there is just one.

Your left hand hides the move.

Watch your left hand to misdirect.

When the audience have seen the grape, take it out. Hold it between your right thumb and finger.

French Drop the grape into your right hand (page 17). Subtly leave the grape in your pocket.

Raise your left hand, and hit the top of your head, letting the grape fall from your mouth.

Take a bite

In this trick, you seem to bite into a china mug, and then mend it by magic.

Before you start the trick, put a broken piece of a hard white mint in your mouth. Hold a coin between your fingers like this.

The clinking sounds like your teeth biting the mug.

Coin

△ 1

To start, pick up a white mug. Hide the coin in your hand, resting on your first finger and squeezed against the mug.

△ 2

Raise the mug to "drink". Press in your second finger, and lift your first finger. The coin clinks on the mug.

The mint looks like a piece of broken china.

△ 3

Pull the mug away, looking astonished that you have broken it, and spit out the mint. Keep the mug tilted in your direction.

△ 4

Look guilty, and rub the "broken" edge with a magic gesture. Then show that the mug has "mended".

Magic banana

To prepare, push a toothpick into a banana and move it side to side. It will cut through the banana without cutting the skin. Do this in several places.

Pick up the banana and make a magic gesture. Then hand the banana to a child to peel. The banana will fall into slices.

Move the toothpick inside the skin.

You could plant the trick banana on the party table, beforehand.

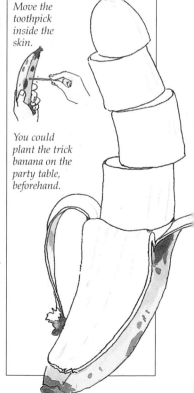

Index

This book is based on material previously published in The Usborne Book of Magic Tricks and The Usborne Complete Book of Magic

First published in 1995 by Usborne Publishing Ltd, Usborne House, 83-85 Saffron Hill, London EC1N 8RT, England.

Copyright © Usborne Publishing Ltd 1989, 1991, 1995.

The name Usborne and the device 🎈 are Trade Marks of Usborne Publishing Ltd.

First published in America March 1996 UE
Printed in Italy.